38
D0433053

HIGH LIFE HIGHLAND AND THE

Mad Grandad THE

Kleptoes

WITHDRAWN

WITHDRAWN

Can YOU spot
the kleptomobile
hidden in the story?

For Susan and Emma; Mad Grandad
wouldn't be the same without them.

Oisín McGann began writing and illustrating stories when he was about six years old. His teachers were very happy about it ... until they discovered that was *all* he wanted to do. When he finished learning all the other things he had to do in school, he went to art college. They were very happy to let him go on making things up ... until they discovered that was all he wanted to do. After college, he had lots of jobs, but kept running into the same problem – people were always making him do other things.

Now he writes and illustrates books for a living ... because it was *all* he ever wanted to do.

Oisín has made up more stuff about Lenny and his grandad in other *Mad Grandad Adventures*.

Mad Grandad AND THE Kleptoes

Oisín McGann

HIGH LIFE HIGHLAND LIBRARIES	
38001800345211	
BERTRAMS	21/08/2018
	£6.50
JF	

This edition first published 2018.
First published 2005 by The O'Brien Press Ltd,
12 Terenure Road East, Rathgar, Dublin 6, D06 HD27, Ireland.
Tel: +353 1 4923333; Fax: +353 1 4922777
E-mail: books@obrien.ie
Website: www.obrien.ie
The O'Brien Press is a member of Publishing Ireland.

ISBN: 978-1-78849-046-7

Copyright for text and illustrations © Oisín McGann
Copyright for editing, typesetting, layout, design
© The O'Brien Press Ltd

All rights reserved. No part of this publication may
be reproduced or utilised in any form or by any means,
electronic or mechanical, including photocopying, recording
or in any information storage and retrieval system,
without permission in writing from the publisher.

1 3 5 7 6 4 2
18 20 22 21 19

Editing, typesetting, layout, design: The O'Brien Press Ltd
Illustrations: Oisín McGann

Printed and bound by CPI Group (UK) Ltd, Croydon, CR0 4YY.
The paper in this book is produced using pulp from managed forests.

Published in

DUBLIN

UNESCO
City of Literature

CHAPTER 1

The Missing Clock

It was Saturday morning, and I
couldn't get into Grandad's house.
There was no **answer** when I knocked.

I looked in the window. Grandad was fast **asleep** in his armchair.

He didn't hear me knocking, so I had to get in through the **dog-flap**. The dog had died years ago, but Grandad had forgotten to get rid of the flap. I trotted into the sitting-room and woke him up.

'Grandad!' I said. 'I was knocking for **ages**!'

'Sorry, lad,' he blinked, and patted me on the head. 'I set my clock to go off before you got here, but it seems to have gone missing again.'

Now, Grandad was a bit mad.
He sometimes heard music in the
chimney, or thought the television
was **watching** him. And whenever
he couldn't wake up in time, he
always said his alarm clock had gone
missing. He even kept spare clocks in
a locked cupboard.

He took another clock out and
wound it up. Then he got me some
orange juice and biscuits from the
kitchen.

I went to turn on the telly.

'Where's the **remote control**,
Grandad?' I asked.

'Oh, it's around somewhere, Lenny,' he said. 'Look under the cushions.'

I couldn't find the control, so I started reading my book instead. Grandad was nodding off in his armchair, so he set his **alarm clock** to wake him in an hour and put it beside him.

CHAPTER 2

They Came from the Sofa

It was very quiet until Grandad started snoring. And then something really **weird** happened.

A small, thin **hand** reached out
from under the cushions of the sofa
and turned off the alarm on the clock.

I crept around behind Grandad's armchair and peered out. The arm disappeared back under the cushions, and there was the sound of **whispering**, like two people arguing quietly.

Then a small **head** slid out from the back of the sofa and looked around. A little, bony creature climbed out and jumped down to the floor. Another one popped out behind it.

They were thin, lumpy and
yellowy-grey, with two arms, **four** legs,
and feet like **hands**. They had beady
eyes and crooked little teeth. They
wore lots of chunky jewellery.

Each little creature pulled a sock
with **eyeholes** down over their heads
and they started creeping around
and picking things up. The taller one
took Grandad's keys, and my book,
but when the short one grabbed
Grandad's glasses, I couldn't stay
quiet any longer.

'Grandad! Wake up!' I yelled as
loud as I could.

Grandad gave a yell as his eyes opened to find a little **monster** standing in front of him.

'We've got a **waker**!' the taller one
shrieked. 'Every Klepto for himself!'

He leapt back over to the sofa,
disappearing down the back of it.
The short one screeched and darted
after him.

I **dived** after the two creatures, and just missed the second one. But I was going so fast when I hit the sofa, I went right in behind the cushions and fell down the back of the sofa.

It was much **bigger** down there than sofas are supposed to be.

CHAPTER 3

Loads of Lost Stuff

I got to my feet and looked around. The place was **huge**, and it was packed with all sorts of stuff. Tunnels led off on every side.

I heard a sliding sound and a
thump, and Grandad landed behind
me.

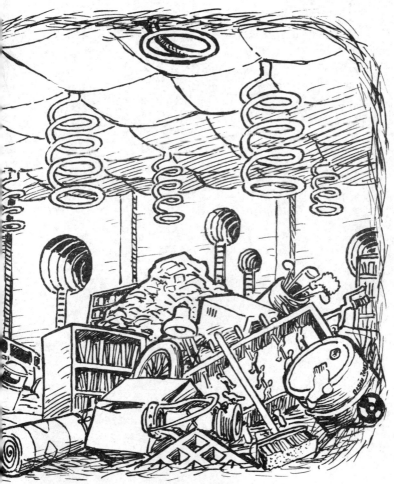

'Holy smoke!' he said when he saw the huge space down the back of his sofa.

'There's your **remote control**,
Grandad,' I said, pointing at the
remote, which sat on a pile of junk.

'You're right, Lenny!' he gasped. 'And there's all my old **alarm clocks**. And my old army boots. And look! Some of my pairs of glasses. I've lost lots of these over the years.'

'You didn't lose them,' I shook my head. 'Those **Kleptoes** stole them.'

Just as I spoke, we heard a twanging sound. The two Kleptoes were making their escape by swinging like monkeys along rows of **springs** hanging from the ceiling. Grandad grabbed one of his old boots, and threw it as hard as he could.

It knocked the taller Klepto to the floor.

I sprinted over and jumped on him. The Klepto started screaming and crying and I got off him, but held onto his arm. He pinched me and pulled my hair with **three** different hands at once.

'Agh!' I yelled, letting go of him.

'Ha ha!' he laughed, and turned to run away, but Grandad seized him by his feet and pulled the **sock** off his head. The Klepto shrieked and hissed at him.

CHAPTER 4

The Klepto Code

'We're not going to hurt you,'
Grandad said to the Klepto, as he held
him up. 'We just want to know **what**
you are. And what you're doing down
the back of my sofa.'

'You don't have to shout! I'm a Klepto. I've got very, very good hearing.'

The skinny creature covered his ears. 'My name's Nickit, and that was my sister, Pinch. That's all I have to tell you. Them's the **Rules**.'

'What rules?' I asked.

'Don't you know anything? It's the **The Klepto Code**,' Nickit snorted.

Rule 1: Steal Everything.

Rule 2: Don't Get Caught.

Rule 3: Don't Talk to Strangers.

Rule 4: Steal Everything.

'You said that last one twice,' I said to him.

'We like that one,' he snapped.

'You can't just go round stealing things,' Grandad growled at him.

'Of course we can,' Nickit sighed. 'We do it all the time. It's easy! You sleep all day – especially when we take your alarm clock! We have to keep robbing them, and we **HATE** alarm clocks.'

Suddenly Pinch, Nickit's sister, appeared out of nowhere and pointed the nozzle of a **vacuum cleaner** at us.

'So that's where my hoover got to,'
Grandad said.

Pinch aimed the nozzle at us and
flicked the switch. Hundreds of hard,
slightly hairy **sweets** blasted out at us.
It was like being hit by stones.

'Aagh!' Grandad cried. 'They've made a gun out of it! Run, Lenny!'

We started to run, but more and more of the sweets stuck to our clothes and our skin. In seconds, we were so covered by sweets, we could hardly move.

Grandad tripped, and rolled down a slope, and I tumbled down after him. We crashed into a stack of shelves holding dozens of **alarm clocks**, and they toppled over on top of us.

CHAPTER 5

Old Mother Klepto

'What's all that noise?' a nasty voice hissed.

We dragged ourselves out from
under the clocks, and scraped the
tacky sweets away. At first, we
couldn't see where the **voice** was
coming from. Then we looked up.

Hanging from a spring above us, was a **huge** creature with loads of arms and legs sticking out of a small, wrinkled body. Evil, squinty eyes stared down at us.

'We stole them, Mammy!' Nickit
called from behind us. 'We stole them
for you!'

'For me?' the Kleptoes' mother cackled. 'Thank you, children! You always know just what to steal for your dear old mother. What lovely **pets** they'll make!'

'You won't make pets of us!'
Grandad shouted, picking something
off the ground.

The creature grabbed him by his
ankle, and hoisted him into the air.

'Don't raise your voice with me, lovey,' she snapped. 'Old Mother Klepto has such sensitive ears. You and this little one will make **darling** pets.'

She snatched me up too, and turned towards an enormous **fish tank** in the corner of the room. She was going to trap us inside!

'Grandad, what do we do?!' I yelped.

'We're getting out of here, Lenny,' he told me.

He was holding an **alarm clock**, and now he wound it up. Mother Klepto saw him do it, and suddenly froze.

'Don't you **dare**!' she hissed.

But Grandad set the alarm and it went off. The evil old monster dropped us, and **cowered** away, covering her ears. We had just enough time to get to our feet, before she bared her teeth and came after us again.

CHAPTER 6

The Old Sofa Goes for Good

We both grabbed some clocks and
started running. The **Kleptoes**
followed us, but we kept setting clocks
and throwing them behind us.

The alarms drove the Kleptoes
mad, and they had to stop and **stamp**
on each one.

We made it to where we had come in. I threw down our last clock and we started climbing. As we clambered out, we heard the ringing stop behind us, and then the **snarling** sound of Old Mother Klepto coming after us.

'Quick, Lenny!' Grandad called, as he picked up his new clock to fend them off. 'Turn on the **stereo**! And turn the volume right up!'

I did like he said, and it worked. The noise kept the Kleptoes inside the sofa. Grandad called some men with a van and we sent that sofa to the dump. We thought the Kleptoes would be **happy** there.

Grandad bought a brand new sofa, and we checked the back of it really **carefully** before it was delivered. Things still go missing sometimes, but as Grandad says; you can't blame the sofa for everything.